Dora's Sleepover

by Lara Bergen
illustrated by Victoria Miller

Ready-to-Read

Simon Spotlight/Nick Jr.

New York   London   Toronto   Sydney

Based on the TV series *Dora the Explorer*® as seen on Nick Jr.®

SIMON SPOTLIGHT
An imprint of Simon & Schuster Children's Publishing Division
1230 Avenue of the Americas, New York, New York 10020
Manufactured in the United States of America
First Edition
2 4 6 8 10 9 7 5 3 1
Library of Congress Cataloging-in-Publication Data
Bergen, Lara.
Dora's sleepover / by Lara Bergen ; illustrated by Victoria Miller. — 1st ed.
p. cm. — (Ready-to-read) (Dora the explorer)
"Based on the TV series Dora the Explorer as seen on Nick Jr."—T.p. verso.
ISBN-13: 978-1-4169-1508-9
ISBN-10: 1-4169-1508-7
I. Miller, Victoria (Victoria H.) II. Dora the explorer (Television program). III. Title. IV. Series.
V. Series: Dora the explorer
PZ7.B44985Dor 2006
2006014520

Hi! I am .

DORA

It is a big night!

I am having a sleepover with my best friend, ,

at his !

First I need to pack .

BACKPACK

Do you see what I should

pack?

I will take my ,
PAJAMAS

my , my ,
FLASHLIGHT   SLEEPING BAG

and my of stories.
BOOK   PIRATE

loves stories!

BOOTS   PIRATE

MAMI has made some **COOKIES** for **BOOTS** and me. Yum! **MAMI** puts the **COOKIES** in a **BASKET**.

Do **you** like ?
COOKIES

Thank you, .
MAMI

Good-bye!

How do we get
to 's ?
BOOTS TREE HOUSE

 can show us
MAP

the way.

We go through the ,

TUNNEL

then through the ,

JUNGLE

and that's how we get to

's .

BOOTS TREE HOUSE

We made it to the .
TUNNEL

But the is so dark!
TUNNEL

Is there something

in my BACKPACK that will

help us see in the dark?

Yeah! A FLASHLIGHT !

We made it through the .
TUNNEL

Now we need to go

through the ![jungle].
JUNGLE

Uh-oh! Do you see

someone behind that ![tree]?
TREE

It is !
SWIPER

 wants to swipe our
SWIPER

 of .
BASKET   COOKIES

Say " , no swiping!"
SWIPER

We stopped .

SWIPER

And there is 's !

BOOTS   TREE HOUSE

We can climb the
LADDER

to get to 's .
BOOTS   TREE HOUSE

Hi, ! I am ready

for our sleepover!

I have my ,
PAJAMAS

my FLASHLIGHT, my SLEEPING BAG,

my BOOK of PIRATE stories,

and a BASKET of COOKIES

from MAMI!

It is time to put on our .

PAJAMAS

Then we can turn on our

 and eat the .

FLASHLIGHTS COOKIES

Yum!

I can read my BOOK

of PIRATE stories

to BOOTS too.

Look at the !
MOON

The is so big and bright.
MOON

 yawns.
BOOTS

 is sleepy.
BOOTS

I am sleepy too.

We get into our .

SLEEPING BAGS

Good night, .

And good night

to you, too!